Yankee Doodle Dandy

BY CALLISTA GINGRICH

ILLUSTRATED BY SUSAN ARCIERO

★ ★ ★ ★ ★ Acknowledgments ★ ★ ★ ★ ★

Thank you to the extraordinary group of dedicated people who made this book possible.

I especially want to thank Susan Arciero, whose superb illustrations have once again brought Ellis the Elephant to life.

The team at Regnery Kids has made writing and publishing *Yankee Doodle Dandy* a real pleasure. Special thanks to Marji Ross, Jeff Carneal, Cheryl Barnes, Diane Reeves, Patricia Jackson, Amanda Larsen, and Jason Sunde for their insightful and creative contributions. Regnery has been remarkable in turning this book into a reality.

My deepest gratitude goes to our staff at Gingrich Productions, including Ross Worthington, Christina Maruna, Bess Kelly, and Woody Hales, whose assistance has been invaluable.

Finally, I'd like to thank my husband, Newt. His enthusiasm for Ellis the Elephant and *Yankee Doodle Dandy* has been my constant source of inspiration.

Cataloging-in-Publication data on file with the Library of Congress
ISBN 978-1-62157-087-5
Published in the United States by
Regnery Kids
An imprint of Regnery Publishing, Inc.
One Massachusetts Avenue NW
Washington, DC 20001
www.Regnery.com

Manufactured in the United States of America
10 9 8 7 6 5 4 3 2 1

Books are available in quantity for promotional or premium use.
Write to Director of Special Sales, Regnery Publishing, Inc., One Massachusetts Avenue NW,
Washington, DC 20001, for information on discounts and terms, or call (202) 216-0600.

Distributed to the trade by
Perseus Distribution
250 West 57th Street
New York, NY 10107

To the patriotic men and women who made
America a free and independent nation.

★ ★ ★ ★ ★

Ellis the Elephant loved America's story,
of freedom won with courage and glory.
He wanted to know how our nation came to be
an independent country, united and free.

In Philadelphia, Ellis read, America got its start,
a bustling city with freedom in its heart.
But even when the Liberty Bell first began to ring,
the American colonies still belonged to the King!

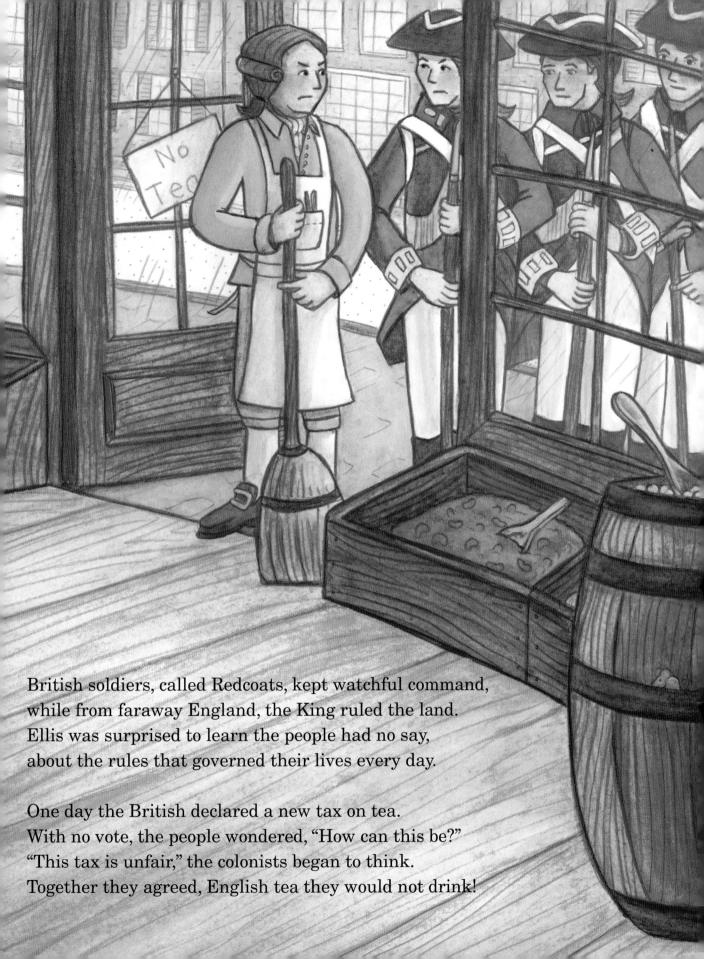

British soldiers, called Redcoats, kept watchful command,
while from faraway England, the King ruled the land.
Ellis was surprised to learn the people had no say,
about the rules that governed their lives every day.

One day the British declared a new tax on tea.
With no vote, the people wondered, "How can this be?"
"This tax is unfair," the colonists began to think.
Together they agreed, English tea they would not drink!

Some thought a boycott was not quite enough.
They wanted to show the King they were tough.
So one night in Boston, ships full of English tea
were raided by the brave Sons of Liberty.

They climbed aboard boats, disguised in the night,
and proclaimed to the King, "This tax is not right!"
They threw the tea overboard into the bay.
The Boston Tea Party is what we call it today.

The King was not amused by the Patriots' games.
He soon made strict rules, only fanning the flames.
"I'll close your port," said the King. "You'll be an example."
"And your new government, I will gladly trample!"

The colonists stood firm and tried not to be scared.
If the King really meant it, they must be prepared.
In Virginia, Patrick Henry saw a revolution ahead.
"Give me liberty or give me death!" he famously said.

In Boston, the Patriots prepared for a fight,
determined to defend their God-given rights.
The Minutemen got ready as tensions grew,
and waited to see what the British would do.

The signal, Ellis learned, would be lanterns, you see.
They'd light "one if by land, and two if by sea."
Then late one night, the Redcoats quietly stirred.
"The British are coming!"—Paul Revere spread the word.

The British marched early before the sun rose,
to Concord to capture the guns of their foes.
The Patriots waited, prepared for attack.
It was clear, Ellis thought, there was no going back!

As the Redcoats marched to the Old North Bridge,
the Minutemen stood on the opposite ridge.
It was here the Revolutionary War came about,
as "the shot heard 'round the world" rang out.

On families, the long, hard war took its toll.
Moms and dads alike played very big roles.
Many Patriots, Ellis was surprised to hear,
were so busy fighting, they weren't home for years.

John Adams' wife, Abigail, was left home alone,
to care for their children and farm on her own.
She wrote many letters to her dear husband John,
sharing advice and cheering him on.

In Philadelphia, the Founding Fathers gathered to proclaim
"All men are created equal, with liberty just the same."
"This," they told the King, "we believe to be true,
our rights come from God—they don't come from you!"

Together the Congress signed a formal Declaration.
The "United States of America" would be its own nation.
This day was very important and now Ellis knew why
we celebrate each year on the Fourth of July!

Ellis learned the new nation would need a flag to fly,
a symbol the people would be proud to hold high.
It was a job Betsy Ross was eager to do,
gladly stitching a banner of red, white, and blue.

The nation's new flag was a sight to be seen,
with a stripe for each colony—the original thirteen.
A circle of stars, each carefully done,
stood for the states, now united as one.

General Washington worried his army would splinter,
as troops settled in at Valley Forge for the winter.
"We're tired," they said. "We're hungry and cold!"
"We want to go home. War has sure gotten old!"

Then Martha Washington and other women too,
arrived at the camp to help pull the troops through.
Soldiers spent the long winter training to win.
It gave them the courage they needed within.

Women joined in as the battle raged on,
and just like the men, they were often quite strong.
Brave Molly Pitcher was ready to fight,
firing cannons with the greatest of might.

At Yorktown, the Patriots built a blockade,
along with the French who sailed to their aid.
And finally the British had to admit,
"The Yankees beat us. It's over. We quit!"

The Redcoats surrendered their swords that day
and readied their ships to take them away.
Ellis was happy all the fighting was done.
The long struggle had ended and freedom had won.

Goodwill ruled the day and the war had ceased.
Britain and the colonies would sign a treaty of peace.
Though the fighting was over, there was work left to do.
Many difficulties still remained between the two.

In Paris they met for the British to concede,
and after long discussions, they finally agreed.
Freeing the colonies, the King let it be known,
the United States was a country of its own.

In their new independence, the people rejoiced,
and searching for a leader, saw an obvious choice.
George Washington was a King they could all get behind.
But to Ellis' surprise, the General politely declined.

"I will not be a King," he said. "It would be a mistake.
I did not defeat the British for a crown to take."
To Mount Vernon he returned, with its quiet fields to roam.
After eight long years of fighting, Washington was home.

America's soldiers then traveled home too.
Their bravery had won our freedom, this Ellis knew.
Returning to their homes, families embraced,
sharing stories of trials and challenges they'd faced.

Ellis remembered those who had sacrificed so much
to create a better life, and he was truly touched.
Now Ellis understood how our independence was won.
With faith, hope, and courage, a new nation had begun.

★ ★ ★ ★ ★ Resources ★ ★ ★ ★ ★

Fun Places to Learn More about the American Revolution

Colonial Philadelphia

By the time of the American Revolution, Phila-delphia, Pennsylvania, was the largest city in the American colonies and an important center of trade. Its most prominent building was the State House, known today as Independence Hall. The famous Liberty Bell, originally cast in 1752, rang from Independence Hall for more than two decades before it sounded during the public reading of the Declaration of Independence on July 8, 1776.

Explore Colonial Philadelphia

Franklin Square ★ *One of Philadelphia's five original public squares, Franklin Square offers one of America's best playgrounds, family fun, and historic storytelling.* ★ *Visit www.historicphiladelphia. org for more information.*

The Liberty Bell Center ★ *The new home of Philadelphia's iconic bell.* ★ *Visit www.nps.gov/inde/ liberty-bell-center.htm for more information.*

Boycott on Tea

In 1767, the British Parliament passed the Townshend Acts, which included a new tax on tea in the American colonies. Colonists, asserting that the British had no right to tax the colonies since they had no representation in Parliament, orga-nized a boycott of English goods, including tea. British troops were stationed in Boston to enforce the Townshend Acts and keep order, leading to heightened tensions between the colonists and the imperial authorities. These tensions boiled over three years later in the Boston Massacre, when several of the troops fired on a crowd of civilians.

Explore Colonial Boston

Faneuil Hall Marketplace ★ *America's first open air marketplace features food, shopping, street theatre, and special events. It is located in the heart of historic Boston.* ★ *Visit www.faneuilhallmarketplace. com for more information.*

★ ★ ★ ★ ★ Resources ★ ★ ★ ★ ★

Fun Places to Learn More about the American Revolution

Boston Tea Party

In 1773, the British Parliament passed the Tea Act in response to the colonials' boycott of tea, effectively reducing the price but keeping the tax in place. When ships carrying a cargo of English tea arrived in Boston Harbor later the same year, colonists protested, demanding the ships not be allowed to unload. An activist group called the Sons of Liberty took matters into its own hands, boarding the ships on December 16, 1773, and dumping the cargo into the bay.

Explore the Boston Tea Party

Old South Meetinghouse ★ *The meeting house where the colonists gathered prior to the Boston Tea Party.* ★ *Visit www.oldsouthmeetinghouse.org for more information.*

Boston Tea Party Ship and Museum ★ *The site where the fateful protest took place. Visit an informative museum and climb aboard one of two authentically restored tea ships.* ★ *Visit www.bostonteaparty ship.com for more information.*

Patrick Henry

Parliament responded to the Boston Tea Party with the so-called "Intolerable Acts," meant to punish the protest by restricting the Massachusetts colonial government. Among other measures, the Intolerable Acts closed Boston's port, brought the colony under the direct rule of a royal governor, and allowed the governor to quarter British troops in privately owned buildings. The acts provoked enormous backlash, not only in Massachusetts, but in the other colonies as well. In a speech to the Second Virginia Convention on March 23, 1775, Patrick Henry responded to the Intolerable Acts and other British abuses by calling on the colonists to raise arms, saying, "I know not what course others may take; but as for me give me liberty or give me death!"

Explore St. John's Church

St. John's Church ★ *See the historic site of Patrick Henry's "Liberty or Death" speech, and possibly catch a reenactment of this famous moment.* ★ *Visit www. historicstjohnschurch.org for more information.*

★ ★ ★ ★ ★ Resources ★ ★ ★ ★ ★

Fun Places to Learn More about the American Revolution

Paul Revere

In April of 1775 the Patriots got word that the British forces in Boston might attempt to confiscate the local militia's supply of weapons stored in nearby Concord, Massachusetts. Late on the night of April 18, 1775, the Patriots learned British troops were preparing to march out of the city. According to a prearranged signal, the colonists hung two lanterns in the steeple of the North Church, indicating the British would cross the Charles River by boat rather than march around Boston Neck by land. Paul Revere, a member of the Sons of Liberty, set out from the city on horseback, alerting every home on the way to Lexington that "the British were coming!"

Explore Paul Revere's Midnight Ride

Old North Church ★ *Located in Boston's North End neighborhood, Old North Church is where Paul Revere received word of the British advance via lanterns displayed in the steeple.* ★ *Visit www.oldnorth. com for more information.*

Paul Revere House ★ *Not far from Old North Church is the preserved home of early America's most famous horseman, Paul Revere.* ★ *Visit www. paulreverehouse.org for more information.*

Battles of Lexington and Concord

The British troops marched from Boston toward Concord, where they suspected Patriot militias had stashed weapons. When they reached the town of Lexington, a skirmish broke out between the British troops and assembled local militia members, killing eight of the Patriots. The British continued to Concord, where they encountered more than four hundred Minutemen near the North Bridge. At some point during the standoff that ensued, historians believe a British regular fired a shot. The American Patriots responded with "the shot heard 'round the world" and sparked a battle that began the American Revolution.

Explore the Battles of Lexington and Concord

Minute Man Visitor Center ★ *Experience the multimedia presentation "The Road to Revolution" to learn about the events which led to the outbreak of America's War for Independence.* ★ *Visit www.nps. gov / mima / planyourvisit / ranger-programs-and-tours.htm for more information.*

North Bridge Visitor Center ★ *After following the "Battle Road" from Lexington, see the site of the "shot heard 'round the world."* ★ *Visit www.nps.gov / mima / index.htm for more information.*

★ ★ ★ ★ ★ Resources ★ ★ ★ ★ ★

Fun Places to Learn More about the American Revolution

Abigail Adams

Abigail Adams was one of the most influential women involved with the American founding. She and her husband, John Adams (a leading Patriot from Massachusetts), exchanged hundreds of letters during the American Revolution. When John was a delegate to the Continental Congresses, Abigail wrote frequently to advise him. As the delegates drafted the Declaration of Independence, she counseled him to make sure the new government would be "more generous and favorable" to the ladies than the last.

Explore the Home of John and Abigail Adams

Adams National Historical Park ★ *Tour the Quincy, Massachusetts, home of John and Abigail Adams.* ★ *Visit www.nps.gov/adam/index.htm for more information.*

Declaration of Independence

On July 4, 1776, the Second Continental Congress met in Independence Hall in Philadelphia to sign the Declaration of Independence, formally separating the colonies from Great Britain. The Declaration listed the colonies' reasons for breaking with the King, and more importantly, expressed the principles on which the United States of America would be founded: "that all men are created equal, that they are endowed by their Creator with certain unalienable Rights, that among these are Life, Liberty and the pursuit of Happiness."

Explore the Signing of the Declaration of Independence

Independence Visitor Center ★ *The best starting point for touring Independence Hall, the Liberty Bell, and the other sites of Independence Mall.* ★ *Visit www.phlvisitorcenter.com for more information.*

National Archives ★ *See the real Declaration of Independence.* ★ *Visit www.archives.gov for more information.*

★ ★ ★ ★ ★ Resources ★ ★ ★ ★ ★

Fun Places to Learn More about the American Revolution

Betsy Ross

Legend has it that in 1776, General George Washington visited Philadelphia seamstress Betsy Ross in her upholstery shop. There, he asked her to sew the first American flag, showing her his sketch of thirteen stars arranged in a circle alongside thirteen red and white stripes. Although no one knows for sure if the story is true, records show that Betsy was paid for making flags just a few weeks before the Congress made this now famous design the official banner of the United States of America.

Explore the Home of Betsy Ross

Betsy Ross House ★ *Learn about life in colonial times at the home of seamstress Betsy Ross, near the heart of historic Philadelphia.* ★ *Visit www.historicphiladelphia.org for more information.*

Valley Forge

In December 1777, General Washington took his army to Valley Forge for the winter encampment. The soldiers were hungry and exhausted when they arrived. Most did not have shoes. They had few supplies to build shelters. Disease was rampant. For the Continental Army, it was one of the bleakest moments of the war. Despite these enormous challenges, however, the soldiers spent hours during the winter at Valley Forge practicing drills under the command of Baron von Steuben, a Prussian military officer introduced by Benjamin Franklin to aid Washington in training the Army.

Explore Valley Forge

Valley Forge National Historical Park ★ *See the place where the Continental Army camped in 1777 for the bleakest winter of the war.* ★ *Visit www.nps.gov/vafo/index.htm for more information.*

★ ★ ★ ★ ★ Resources ★ ★ ★ ★ ★

Fun Places to Learn More about the American Revolution

Molly Pitcher

The lore of the American Revolution includes the story of "Molly Pitcher," whose function with the Army included carrying water to the troops. When Molly's husband was wounded in battle, she is said to have taken his place, helping to fire the artillery. The real "Molly Pitcher" is thought to have been Mary Hays of Pennsylvania, whose husband, William Hays, was injured in the Battle of Monmouth. Molly Hays had joined her husband during the winter at Valley Forge and later followed him into combat, assisting the troops.

Explore the Battle of Monmouth

Monmouth Battlefield State Park ★ *See where the legendary Molly Pitcher is said to have made her heroic stand during one of the Revolutionary War's largest battles.* ★ *Visit www.state.nj.us/dep/ parksandforests/parks/monbat.html for more information.*

Yorktown

In the autumn of 1781, the war at last reached its decisive moment in Yorktown, Virginia. There, General Washington and Rochambeau, the commander of the French forces, converged on the British Army. Around the same time, the French naval fleet arrived to prevent the British from retreating by sea. After one final battle, General Cornwallis conceded defeat. He surrendered on October 19, 1781.

Explore the Battle of Yorktown

Yorktown Victory Center ★ *Located in Virginia's Historic Triangle, Yorktown is where the United States finally won its independence.* ★ *Visit www. historyisfun.org for more information.*

★ ★ ★ ★ ★ Resources ★ ★ ★ ★ ★

Fun Places to Learn More about the American Revolution

Treaty of Paris

On September 3, 1783, the United States and Great Britain signed the Treaty of Paris, officially ending the American Revolution. In Paris, France, John Adams, Benjamin Franklin, and John Jay represented the United States at the negotiations with representatives of the King. By signing the Treaty, Britain formally recognized the United States as a free and independent country and ceded enormous territory in the west to the new nation.

Explore the Maryland State House

Maryland State House ★ *Visit the place where the Treaty of Paris was ratified in the United States, officially ending the Revolutionary War. The Maryland State House is also where General Washington resigned his commission as Commander in Chief of the Continental Army.* ★ *Visit www.visitannapolis. org for more information.*

Mount Vernon

After the war, many wanted to appoint George Washington King, but instead, he appeared before the Congress and resigned his commission as Commander in Chief. He then returned home to his Virginia estate, Mount Vernon. Upon hearing this news, Washington's former adversary King George III remarked that if true it would make Washington "the greatest character of the age." In fact, the General longed to return home. During the eight-year war, he had made only one brief visit to Mount Vernon. He remained there as a private citizen until 1789, when he was elected unanimously as the first president of the United States.

Explore Mount Vernon

Mount Vernon ★ *George Washington's home and plantation is one of America's greatest and most educational historic sites.* ★ *Visit www.mountvernon. org for more information.*

Soldiers' Homecoming

Like their General, the soldiers laid down their arms following the war and disbanded. Tens of thousands of these soldiers had fought to win independence, many for years at a time. They faced many new challenges as they returned to life as private citizens. In the years ahead, they would work together to form a new Republic—an experiment in liberty unlike anything the world had ever seen.